This book
belongs to:

Or would you go to the city, be friend
fountain in it, travel by rickshaw, eat
and a deer-stalker hat, keep a pet touc
for fun and sleep in a bunk bed? Or w
ghost, live in a wigwam with a trampoli
and mash, wear a denim jacket with a
fashion model, blow bubbles and s
the seaside, be friends with a Viking, li
in it, travel by limousine, eat a box of c
hat and fluffy mules, keep a pet eleph
and sleep in a kennel? Or would you go
a tower block with a secret door in it,
a poncho with stilettos and a furry h
line-dancing and sleep on a camp-bed?
be friends with an alien, live in a lig
canoe, eat a bag of crisps, wear a kilt
a pet unicorn, be an astronaut,

vith a pirate, live in a spaceship with a
ter, wear a suit of armour with trainers
be a deep-sea diver, build a snowman
l you go to the moon, be friends with a
in it, travel by paddle boat, eat sausages
a and wedges, keep a pet monkey, be a
p in a shoe? Or would you go to
in a fairy palace with a ping-pong table
olates, wear a grass skirt with a cowboy
be a hairdresser, go on a bouncy castle
a desert, be friends with a knight, live in
el by helicopter, eat a hamburger, wear
keep a pet spider, be a magician, go
would you go to the top of a mountain,
ouse with chandeliers in it, travel by
h winkle-pickers and a sombrero, keep
jigsaw and sleep in a hammock?

In memory of Henry Brown
N. S.

To everyone at Browsers Bookshop
P. G.

YOU CHOOSE
A PICTURE CORGI BOOK 978 0 552 54708 6

Published in Great Britain by Picture Corgi Books,
an imprint of Random House Children's Books

Doubleday edition published 2003
Picture Corgi edition published 2004

9 10

Picture Corgi Books are published by
Random House Children's Books,
61–63 Uxbridge Road, London W5 5SA,
a division of The Random House Group Ltd,

Addresses for companies within The Random House Group Limited
can be found at : www.randomhouse.co.uk/offices.htm

THE RANDOM HOUSE GROUP
Limited Reg. No. 954009
www.**rbooks**.co.uk

A CIP catalogue record for this book is available from the British Library.

Printed in Singapore

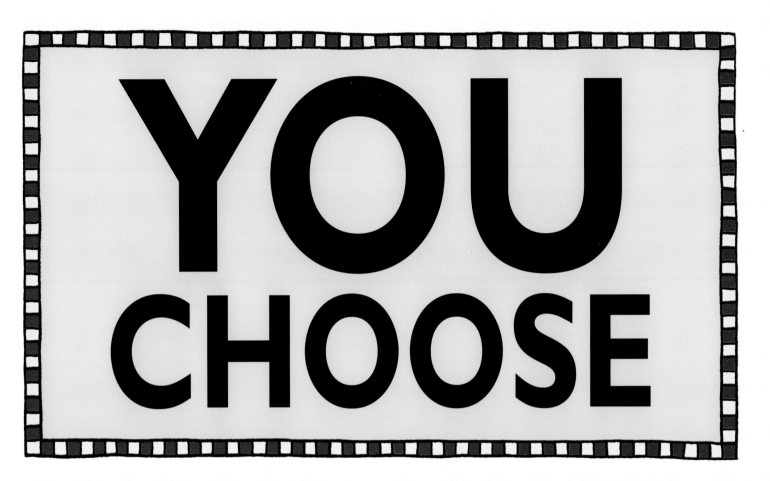

Words by Pippa Goodhart, pictures by Nick Sharratt

Picture Corgi

If you could go anywhere,

where would you go?

Who would you like for

family and friends?

What kind of home

would you choose?

Would you travel with wheels or wings?

Or perhaps choose one of these other things?

what would you eat?

Choose some shoes ...

...and perhaps a hat?

Why not get yourself a pet...

or two or three or more?

Is there a job

you'd like to do?

What would you do...

...for fun?

And when you got tired and felt like a snooze,

where would you sleep? You choose. Goodnight!

Or would you go to the desert, be f
caravan with a drum set in it, travel by
with flip-flops and a furry hat, keep a
for fun and sleep in a cradle? Or would
live in a cave with a swimming pool in
wear a tuxedo with Roman sandals and
go on a roller coaster and sleep in
outer space, be friends with a baby,
on it, travel by steam train, eat a waterm
lacy boots, keep a pet polar bear,
and sleep in a hammock? Or would you
live in a cottage with a secret door in i
wear a kilt with clogs and a top
birdwatching and sleep on a nest? Or
be friends with a vampire, live in a tree
space shuttle, eat squid, wear a bow-tie
a pet bat, be a deep-sea diver, re

ds with Superwoman, live in a gypsy hip, eat sponge cake, wear a feather boa dragon, be a clown, make phone calls go to the seaside, be friends with a wolf, travel by helicopter, drink milkshakes, nnet, keep a pet lizard, be an astronaut, bed of flowers? Or would you go to e on a toadstool with a glitter light n, wear dungarees with a sailor's hat and e an architect, go bungee jumping to the moon, be friends with a gangster, avel by paraglider, eat corn-on-the-cob, keep a pet panda, be a pilot, go uld you go to the top of a waterfall, use with a rocking horse in it, travel by th ballet shoes and a panama hat, keep a book and sleep in a space-bed?

More books to choose from . . .

Written by Pippa Goodhart:
Slow Magic
illustrated by John Kelly

Pam's Maps
illustrated by Katherine Lodge

Illustrated by Nick Sharratt:
Shark in the Park
written and illustrated by Nick Sharratt

Pants
written by Giles Andreae

The Daisy Books
Eat Your Peas
Really, Really
You Do!
Yuk!
If I Was Boss
A Bunch of Daisies
written by Kes Gray